*To Paul
all love*

Half Term, High Tide Belligerent Ghouls Run Schools

For Miss Smith
Maybe I've forgotten the name and the address,
Of everyone I've ever Known,

> *With that I've no regrets,*
> *Save it for another day,*
> *It's the school exams,*
> *The kids have ran away.*
> *[New Order, Regret]*

Chapter 1 School in the 1980s

Rob grew up in on a council estate in Leicester. A large sprawling estate in the Western Suburbs that was built at the end of the war as homes for heroes with hot and cold running water, inside toilets, gardens and the infrastructure of Schools, shops and health centres, God bless Bevan!

Milton Keynes it wasn't but there was a diverse cross section of the working classes and the education system had progressed through the unfair grammar school/11 plus system and the damned secondary modern and technical schools to the comprehensive system and New Parks Boys' School, whilst ran upon grammar school lines was in every way comprehensive. Rob's Dad would tell him about his 11 plus exam

Both the secondary modern and comprehensive were very much ran along the values and disciplines of the grammar and public school system but by the 1980s some schools like Countesthorpe College had adopted liberal ideas like non -school uniforms and calling their teachers by their Christian names.

New Parks Boys' School did not adhere and subscribe to the new liberal ideas. The wooden veneer entrance hall was full of sporting pictures of first XVs of years gone by. Black and white and colour photographs of old boys with long hair and Clopper Castle haircuts. Cabinets full of sporting silver cups and plates for rugby, football and athletics. Huge lists of head boys and headmasters and the school motto, 'Rejoicing in Truth'.

The school building was an early fifties brick build in an H shape. The girls' school stood next door in a perfect geometric mirror. Bizarrely enough the old grammar school that had been in operation for 300 years [Alderman Newton's School]1 had been relocated from the centre of Leicester to next door in the 1970s!

There was a tradition of many secondary schools in Leicester not being co-educational in the 1970s and early 80s but costs forced amalgamations with pace after the mid-decade. New Parks Boy's School was ran with pride and tradition, discipline was a key feature.

On Rob's first day in his crisp black uniform and kipper tie, he was told in no uncertain way about the rules by fearsome straight faced [no smile until year 11 teachers]. He was lucky he got Haddon the Goodun as a form tutor, his brother Haddon the Baddun was also a teacher and had a fearsome reputation. Haddon the Goodun was still strict and old fashioned but as students they knew he cared.

The school was ran with 5 separate houses names after prominent Britons. Bannister, Cheshire, Hilary, Scott and Whittle and consequently had a 5 form intake. The teachers set their stall out from the off. 'Walk on the left in, form captain at the front! Blazers on at all times, stand up when a member of staff enters the room'.

Punishments were harsh. I was caned along with Mark Vickers by Mr Greenhaugh for giggling in English. Phillip Lay who wore his brother's hand me downs was ragged around the classroom by an angry Maths teacher and Mr King the science teacher had special treatments! Mr King would light tapers and get the student to hold them between their fingers before hitting them out with his cane. Another treat was drawing a chalk number in reverse in his shoe. He would then whack the student upon the bottom and the number would be perfectly reproduced on the pupil's black trousers.

It was evident, even back then that schools were underfunded. The desks were ancient, covered in graffiti from years before. The desk lids were screwed down. The school pens were bic blue plastic with white bulbous ends and hurt one's fingers. They were cheap and robust. The school toilets were grim and leaked. They were imported from Dachau.

The differences from Primary school were huge. You lost your first name for five years at secondary school. There were cries down the corridor of 'You Boy!' You had a timetable and went to specialist teachers and did new exciting subjects like woodwork. Mr Roth scared the kids in his safety talk about Fatty being stabbed by Skinny whilst messing around with a file. Consequently, everyone laughed at the class fat kid. Bullying was covertly encouraged in a character forming way, a bit like the Hitler Jugend.

Assemblies started every week and there was an update of the weekend's sporting fixtures. Hymns were sung and Mark Vickers was often pulled out to the front with other boys for not singing and made to stand in front on the stage! In fact Rob and Mark were actually pulled out of St Aiden's Easter service by Mr Murkitt for laughing. The boys did steal the hymn books to go carol singing for money around the wealthy Letchworth Road area which they also fleeced for trick or treat.

Sport was a huge feature of the school and Rob played both rugby and football. The fixtures took place on Saturday mornings and it was not until the teacher strikes of the late 80s that this stopped. The school grew some very good sportsmen; the Heggs brothers, Ian Dunoon and Dean Yates all getting professional football contracts. Rob himself played for Westleigh Rugby Club in the National Divisions. The school sports teams excelled. There was a bullish pressure to have character and be a good sportsman. In year 7 once the teacher Mr Owens who was also refereeing the rugby match stuck his head into the scrum and said to the prop 'Gibson you're crap!'

Rob's rugby team had some very talented players who if continued would have made club and possibly country players. Mark Vickers was an athletic and aggressive number 8, Tim Spence a great footballer and talented fly half. Gary Heathcote and Mark Miller in the centres, pretty boys who could play and of course Rob, a naturally gifted player with both skill and natural knowledge and instinct. One huge mistake he made was changing position to second row and back row; he was never fast enough but as a loose head prop he could have made it all the way to the top[if he overcame his lack of self-esteem].

Showers were a strange experience. No one wanted to get naked and be observed by Mr Warner in the showers. The kids were forced to have them and watched. Rob once just put his hair under and was forced back in by Warner. Odd really because after school Rob couldn't wait to get into the large rugby baths after a game with 30 other blokes!

The style of education was very much chalk and talk and worksheet based. The books were always well marked and lessons were engaging. The boys daren't be disengaged! For those students who had educational needs they went to special classes and were officially called the Remedials. They became commonly known as the Remedies and were ran by Mr Ben, a huge black man.

The school was amalgamated in year 9 and automatically Rob's peer's behaviour changed. Camaraderie was lost and the lads started acting as peacocks. Vickers started dating a girl called Maria and lived his perverse dreams by passing chewed up sandwiches and chocolate bars from mouth to mouth on the bus with her. The only girls that Rob and Vickers had met before were Andrea Smithson and Jenny. One Sunday afternoon Vickers and Sutton were walking around Western Park in their Italian Combat Jackets bought from Irish Menswear and they also had Fred Perry Polo shirts done up to the neck underneath. Jenny and Andrea. The girls were from the affluent Hilder's Road but they wound the lads up calling them Posh.

School fashion was odd because there was little room for individuality. This was confined to footwear, crossovers and quilites, bowling shoes and Docs. Haircuts, wedges and flicks, long haired Grebos such as Wayne Smith who had home drawn Indian Ink and pin Status Quo and Black Sabbath tattoos at the age of 11. Bags were also one way of showing fashion sense. Adidas holdalls then later Head Bags. Also canvas army bags with marker pen graffiti. RS 4 AG TLA, The Who, The Jam was on Rob's bag at one stage. Nadine Dunn had Tears for Fears on her blue canvas bag and she was cool with her flick haircut and resting solemn angular face.

School trips were an experience. There was the options of a narrow boat trip, a week in the Lake District or Snowdonia. Rob went for a week in the Lakes in year 8 with Vickers and the year 9s. There was a tuck shop behind a hatch that lifted up and a young Cumbrian lad about 18 operated it. Fishcake in year 9 wrote you are a wanker on a piece of paper and stuck it up on one side so when the guy opened his hatch the message popped down in his face, with the writing the correct way up. Upon reading his note the lad called the Youth hostel boss who along with a teacher questioned Fishcake who had owned up to the heinous crime. 'What is a wanker? asked the boss. Fishcake replied nodding at the kid 'He is'.

By the time the students were in year 10 and 11 they were treated like adults. The teachers went the extra mile and Mrs Ducksbury the English teacher made Steinbeck's Of Mice and Men be as human and soulful and relevant as it should be. Mr Lightly a Geordie who was terrifying in year 7 set the scene for lifelong learning. It was in this environment Rob decided that he wanted to work in. But he was a long way off with his 5 O'levels. At the time the brainy kids did O'Levels and the others did CSE's, by the late 1980's this was thought of as elitist and consequently replaced by GCSEs. In the GCSE system A-C was a good pass and D to F a bad pass. So the government created yet another elitist system to beat kids and teachers with, especially with tiered entry in some subjects.

Chapter 2

Rob was working at the CO-OP Dairy on Glenfield Road in Leicester, a huge red brick Victorian building with Faroe Island brickwork. It was built with pride, even though it was a functional workplace it had subtle gothic designs and art deco tiling. Rob was taken aback on his first day by the noise, a million milk bottles jostling for position, clanking and screaming. The noise of the machines, growling and grumbling and the overpowering stale smell of milk and steam. The dairy employed all sorts of people of all ages. It employed green card holders who had some sort of learning difficulty whose jobs were to watch the empty milk bottles and pick out the foreign bodies that the washer and magic eye failed to see.

Johnny Loveland had worked there since school and he was now 63 and had a huge handlebar moustache. Rob called him Jonny Love Juice. He was as mad as a box of frogs and once stripped off in the changing rooms and left the dairy and tried to make his way home to Saffron Road just in his wellies.

Austin was another 'odd leg' everyone knew him as Oggy. As he watched the bottles intently Rob would shout at him. 'Oi Oggy!' Oggy would look up and Rob would make a gesture to him with his two fingers and eyes and reply 'Keep your eyes on the job'.Oggy would go crackers and throw empty milk bottles or brushes at Rob.

Rob's first job in the dairy was stacking the cartons that were shrink wrapped at the end of the line onto pallets. Eight hours of lifting and bending down. The hot heat sealed plastic burnt his palms and gave him callouses. Big Esau who had also started and was also a bouncer said that it was much better than working at Bungey Richard's Foundry.

Rob soon progressed to the four pint machine where he met Jonny Jones. He was an interesting character about 7 years older than the 19 year old Rob. He had just come out of the army and he kept Falcons as a hobby. He was funny and Rob bonded with him. Rob often played practical jokes on Jonny and once unscrewed Jonny's car's licence plate and screwed it to the four pint machine.

Rob was now in a serious relationship with Miranda and he worked for a whole year without a day off, not Saturday or Sunday or holidays. He had amassed a small fortune in overtime and he bought the best clothes that Limeys and The End sold. Armani, Chipie, Ralph Lauren, Boneville.

He bought himself an Opel Manta GTE car and used his money for travel. Miranda and Rob had some amazing holidays. Florida, where Rob couldn't drive because he was just 19. The space and the food blew Rob away. The excitement of the theme parks and seeing Alligators at the side of the road. Driving on Daytona Beach and the cool air conditioned shopping malls where Rob snapped up Paul Weller export compact discs.

Jamaica was a huge experience for the couple. Land crabs at night walking around the hotel grounds, crazy cocktails and Red Stripe Beer, Curried Lobster and Goat and the fireflies at night. Walking outside the hotel there was a shack with a makeshift bar and rows of speakers, enough for a Rolling Stone's concert. Rob and Miranda went inside and the Reggae boomed. They were the only two in there. The next day the barman collared them 'Great Party last night man!' One day a guy came running out of the bushes near the beach offering to cook at his restaurant 'Best Food man'. So Rob agreed to meet him on the beach where he was going to take them to his restaurant.

At 7pm Rob and Miranda met the guy on the beach only to find his restaurant was the beach. He had cool boxes and a fire and blankets. Bizarrely enough the rice and curried shrimp was awesome.

The couple went to Gambia in Africa and baboon monkeys chased Miranda and stole her Benneton duffle bag. There was a military coup and a soldier pointed a rifle at Rob one afternoon down a rural path. Rob just stared at him and that was enough for the soldier to put the rifle down and walk on. There was the strange world of ex-pats that they became invited to, secret colonial clubs where exquisite dinner was served by black waiters and gin and tonics in crystal tumblers. The craziest thing about Banjul was the Croc' pool. A pool in the village centre where the villagers worshipped a live crocodile. There was also the idea that if you took the villager's photograph you stole their soul.

Anstey Rugby Club actually had their own language. This was derived from Mark Vickers who always got his words mixed up. For example a bottle of Pils became a bickle of pols. Newcastle Brown Ale was nuclear brown. A soda syphon was a cider sophon and the boxers Nigel Benn and Evander Holyfield were Lavender Holly bush and Tony Benn.

The pub The Hare and Hounds became known as the Hairy Dewberry and The Savoy was the Savaloy. In the changing rooms before games Bill, Reuben and Butler would all smoke, this was known as tab on. The Anstey players could have walked into any of the county first teams but stayed loyal and over achieved for their small club. Awesome tough players like Julian, who was a polymath player as hard as Swithland Slate but the nicest guy to his friends. He could go on and talk a bit and once a ref' said to him 'Number 3 you're boring', meaning boring in to his opposition in the scrum. Rasper loved this and used to say it all the time using the boring word for its other meaning.

Rugby was great for brotherhood. During his time at Old Newts' RFC Rob met an inspirational character called Tony Bennet. A mulleted hair, good looking character. An awesome fly half and leader. He played fly half and was as funny and cheeky on the pitch as off. He once checked the Referee's boots studs after he's checked the teams. On leading songs after the game, he was the master. At Coventry Saracens. A club with its ground in the middle of a council estate and focus of the estate. Tony led a sing song which crescendo in him getting naked and tucking his manhood between his legs to 'hasn't she got a hairy mutt'.

His brother Steve was such a muscular, nightmare of a scrum half that he had worn away his cup and ball joint on his shoulder through such hard tackling by the age of 25! It was around this time that Rob met Nottingham Paul. He was a true raver and he took Rob to clubs like Deluxe and The Garage in Nottingham, after he'd scored his ecstasy, speed and sometimes Coke from St Ann's.

A large transvestite bouncer always put a lollypop in Rob's mouth when he went to The Garage. One night after The Garage they went too hot to Trot in Mansfield. To get into the club one had to call a number a week before to register. This particular night Rob ended up talking to Boy George in the toilets. He was djing there and he was very polite and pleasant to Rob. As the night wore on, the drugs began to work. Rob stood dead in the middle of the dancefloor as there was a beeping noise. He looked at Paul.
Paul said 'don't worry, I've got this tune on tape'. They carried on dancing. After about ten minutes a bouncer approached them.
'What are you two muppets doing? Get out. Can't you hear the fire alarm?'
Rob realised he needed to do something with his life. One night after going to Deluxe with Paul and dropping half an E, Rob drove home in his XR2. It was a clear night and nothing was on his mind. As he left the slip road and entered the quiet dual carriageway of the A46 road from Nottingham to Leicester he could see 2 bright lights at the top of the hill. Rob thought that they were roadworks.

One of the lights sped off into the night sky at supersonic speed and the other light flew and stopped above Rob's car. Rob went faster and slower and it was still there. He stopped and opened his window and looked up, expecting it to be a Police Helicopter. No noise, just the rustling of the hedges at the side of the road. The light was about 100 feet above him and silent. Rob sped off, he was doing 120 miles an hour and it was still with him. When he got to the Durham Ox Hotel, a lorry passed on the other side of the dual carriage way and the light was gone. Rob got in to his house at Syston and looked out across the fields and into the sky from his bedroom window. Miranda stirred 'What the Hell are you doing?'
'You're never gonna believe this Mirand'. Was his reply.
Rob never knew if it was real or imagined. Nelly and The Dove used to go to a club in Birmingham called Wobble. These guys took acid and thought it will be legalised. Rob and Steve went once and dropped some. It was a nightmare. They were on the same trip. Every time Steve pulled back the black curtain on the wall, they were both in a plane looking outside of the window.

It got worse with the curtain shut everything was normal. But if they turned around to go to the toilet, it was like being on a motorway and flashing lights sped towards them. To go to the toilet or to egress the building the pair had to walk backwards.

In the end the Cow lads would not let Steve or Rob take any gear because they went crazy and were a liability. They would rag people around and be totally out of control. Once Steve ragged around and threw one of Leicester's top gangsters around the Mosquito Coast Club.

Chapter 3

Rob knew he had to change his life. He was now working for Nestle in a warehouse, picking boxes, bored out of his gourd. One day he went to a Choices Centre in Leicester and got details on how to enrol for a degree. This involved doing a foundation course with the Open University. Rob enrolled and consumed himself in the course. He worked every night and attended every lecture. He excelled and passed every essay. He loved learning about Philosophy, Art History, Literature and History.

Rob rang in sick and went to The Tate art gallery, he immersed himself into Ford Maddox Brown and Rossetti. Rob knew every brush stroke in Pegwell Bay and every Character in Work. He knew Maddox Brown's work more than he knew the characters on the album cover of Sgt Pepper's Lonely Hearts Club Band was a changed man. He studied Spenser's Fairy Queen and Hard Times by Dickens. He was amazed by Pugin and Darwin's private notes. Rob was so consumed he forgot that Miranda also made sacrifices for Rob, both monetary and time. With his foundation degree passed, Rob enrolled on a degree course with Leicester University. He worked every day and attended lectures in the evenings. His lecturer was Ron Greenhall. A Salford man who captured Rob with his views on less eligibility of the poor. Work Houses and the Poor Law. Greenhall was a lifelong learner and Rob worshipped him. Greenhall loved towns and cities and their morphology. He hated trees being planted in streets and was often out spoken.

After 5 long years Rob graduated with a real degree! He thought everything would change but these things take time. Rob decided that he wanted to teach, he figured that he loved his subject so much, what could be better than talking about it for 8 hours? He had loved his experience at school so it would be win, win. Rob applied to the University of Nottingham to undertake the yearlong Postgraduate Certificate in Education. His interview was in Lenton in November and he was due to begin the course the following September. He would not get any money and this worried Miranda. They lived in the best area of Syston in a detached house, they had nice holidays to Venice, Florence and America. They would lose all this. The death knell was when Rob attended a Morrissey concert at Nottingham Rock City on the 8th of November.

At this point of 1999 Morrissey did not have a record contract but he was on tour to small venues in the UK and USA. He hadn't appeared live for ages and the tour was a bit of a secret, not being advertised. Rob agreed to go with a girl from work called Melon. The atmosphere at the gig was electric, the anticipation was as high as Everest and was building and building. Rock City was dark and sweaty and rammed beyond capacity with the largely male audience. Some gigs are male dominated and they even open the ladies' toilets in order to accommodate this. Ian Brown, Oasis, Charlatans are all such. Morrissey hit the stage with Boy Racer and the crowd went mad with desire. He wore a West Ham Boys' Club t shirt and this was removed and thrown into the crowd. Melon and Rob were swept along with the euphoria. Probably a little too much as they ended up on her couch removing her black see through Calvin Klein bra in Whitwick. That was it Rob was hooked. He thought that he was honest and had integrity and being with Melon was the correct thing to do as they liked the same music and fashion. In reality it was Miranda that he should have showed the integrity to. He was romanticising as if Melon and him were like Stuart Sutcliffe and Astrid.

He was in love, he did not eat for weeks and lost 3 stone in weight until he had the courage to tell Miranda and leave. Change is the theme of life and this was a huge period of change after years of calm. Christmas came and the couple spent it in Newquay where rob found his other love, Surfing. New Year's Eve 2000 was spent on Beacon Hill with champagne and they looked at the sparkling lights flickering away in Loughborough and the tiny fireflies of the fireworks flying into the air in the valley miles below. Melon wore a trench coat with nothing underneath. She was obsessed with Rob. She showered Rob with compliments and gifts and her body.

Chapter 4

Easter came and a pre-requisite to the PGCE Rob had to spend two weeks in a Primary School. He chose his old school, New Parks House Primary. It stood in the middle of the huge council estate and its pre-war red brick construction was functional and imposing. The school was in special measures. Rob had no idea what this meant.

On his first day he entered the school through the main doors and the smell took him back to 1979. Everything was much smaller than he remembered. He was shown around by the new executive head and the hall brought back the ghosts and echoes of the past. Lizzy Miller pulling his hair, Andrea Martin and her long blonde hair, Paul Bunney and playing marbles and conkers with David Moulds. There was one teacher there left who had taught Rob. Here name was Mrs Cooke and she remembered him fondly. It was so obvious now that she was a lesbian, she was a rugby fan and foretold Rob that he'd be a good rugby player.

Mr Brown was the teacher that Rob was to sit with for the next two weeks. He was about 40 and friendly. He was very professional and he was firm with the children. He showed Rob his lesson plans and told how he worked all day every Sunday planning. The kids were well behaved for him. On a Thursday he had planning time and the children were so naughty for the cover teacher, it was like chalk and cheese.

Some of the children would grab out at Rob's hand, often to be led out or in for break time. At the end of the first week Rob noticed that between his fingers he had itchy red marks. The only thing that would stop them itching was putting them in red hot water. Rob was now living in Melon's wonderful show home in Whitwick, complete with new conservatory!

He asked Melon if she had changed the washing powder. She hadn't. On the Sunday he went to the Red Cow pub and showed Cog his hands.

'Look here Cog, at the state of my hands, they itch like a tramp's vest'.

'You know what that is mate? We get it on the Post. It's called Scabies, they are little mites that live in your skin'.

Mr Brown explained to Rob about the significance of Free School Meals and data and results. Rob had no idea and was appalled at how this was stereotyped and used. Mr Brown emphasised his catchment by getting them to do a questionnaire about how many books there were in their houses.

Rob was still working at Nestle which enabled him to have some disposable income. At the end of May, he took Melon to Ibiza for the weekend. They went on spec' and door knocked until they found a hotel with vacancies.

It was a great break. Sunsets at Mambo and Savannah. Judge Jools in the dj booth. A clockwork orange and old hippies. Coke bought on the strip which was washing powder for 50 Euros.

They went to the white ancient Ibiza Town. Had black Paella and Sangria for lunch. In the afternoon they walked along the old walls and looked out to sea. Rob stood behind her and she pulled up her long flowing dress and undid his fly from behind and guided him into her as she leant over the wall looking out to sea.

In late June Rob went to Benidorm for 3 days with Steve and the Red Cow lads. They were more mature now and affluent and stayed in the Sol Pelicanos. Some things never change and Rob, Steve and Dave threw fruit at busses below from their balcony!

Rob slept with 4 women in 3 days, he was now 30 years old and for some reason he had become attractive to the opposite gender.

Steve spent most of his days in the peep show booths.

The summer wore on and in September it was time for Rob to leave Nestle as he was to start his PGCE. The last day at work was to be followed with a trip to Croydon that night to meet the London team. Kerry the office girl had booked Rob and her a train.

On the train Kerry showed Rob her new lacy thong underwear, which he thought was a bit odd. It all became clear that after the drunken night in Croydon, she slipped into Rob's bed. Rob was excited and nervous as he arrived at the Jubilee Campus at the University of Nottingham. There were the usual introductory speeches and how we were lucky to be at the University as it's a proper uni not an old poly and is in the top 6.

Rob met his course peers. There were 29 of them of all ages. Some of the younger ones openly said that they were only doing the course to get another year at Uni after their masters. Rob was aggrieved at this.

The University days were spent looking at how to make worksheets and practical information. Rob's first placement was at the Rural Keyham School. The kids were so well behaved that they could teach themselves. The staffroom had a shed within it for smoking and the staff looked all tired and miserable. Rob was given the task by Mr Williams the Head of History of sorting through the old worksheets in the filing cabinet. The paper was so old that it was sticky and cold. It was paper that could have been vellum. Most lessons were chalk and talk and worksheets. Rob's 1971 VW Beetle took him there every day and in reality he learnt nothing. The highlight was the French teacher asking Rob out!

Christmas came and Melon and Rob spent it in New York. The flights were horrendous and people were screaming at the turbulence on the plane. The snow was deep in New York and they walked for hours to get to Times Square and see Muhammad Ali bring in 2001. They stopped at the trendy W Hotel in Manhattan and saw all of the sites. Rob made a special visit to the Dakota Building to see where John Lennon had been shot. Rob realised that he had the same Pea coat on that he wore in St Petersburg in Russia with Miranda just a year earlier. He loved Russia, the snow was thick and their breath froze on their faces. He felt that he's achieved something when he got off the train at the Finland Station. The Pet Shop Boys mentioned the Station in West End Girls. Change, life is resilience and change.

A new year and a new placement. This time in East Leake. Rural and top of the school's league tables. Rob taught properly here. Phil Renshaw was the Head of History and he was a Svengali figure to Rob. He never shouted at the students and always spoke calmly to them. Phil was also a great fly half and played for Nottinghamians RFC. Rob started to play for East leake RFC with the head of Geography and he was back to playing at his best.

Rob learnt things about schools and himself. He found set 1 to be aloof and entitled but they did identify with Rob as he was a nice guy and knew his subject. Set 2's are problematic, often as intellectual as set 1 but are frustrated by the setting and are naughty, mostly with low level behaviour problems. Rob liked his set 3 class and they loved him. He was observed by OFSTED with them and they performed loyally for him, all putting their hands up. They were proper kids, wanting to do well but a bit rough around the edges and a bit jaded by the setting system. Rob was also a proper bloke and not a careerist or a pedagogist or a middle class moron.

Any set below set 3 was the forlorn hope. Nice kids but dim. Compliant as they often were not clever enough to misbehave like set 2.

Rob also noticed how mad some teachers were and how they craved adulation or control. For charity the Head teacher went on a sponsored swim around the school with snorkel, goggles and flippers. He wandered around the corridors pretending to swim. Rob looked at the teachers reactions. The normal teachers though 'knob', the creeps and careerists cheered him on. It was his show not a school.

Rob still had to attend university once in a while but this wound him up as all it seemed to be was 'let's talk about what we did last week in schools'.

Rob passed his written assignments and his in school observations. He had to do a school based project for 6 weeks. Mad Helen from Chesterfield talking him into working with her. They did an experiment based upon diet and academic results. They gave kids at Sutton School breakfast and tested them and different types of food and tested them. However, most of Helen and Rob's time was spent in the coffee shop in MacArthur Glen.

Rob began to apply for jobs and as he was spending more and more time in Cornwall surfing he thought that he should move there. He had interviews from Hayle [handy for Phelps's Pasties] to Newquay. He had a two day interview in Jersey, which he had to fly to. However, he accepted a job on the coast in Norfolk.

Rob's house sale with Miranda had gone through and although she had no reason to be fair, she gave Rob half. He now had £25 grand in the bank. Not being selfish at all he decided to circumnavigate the world at the end of his PGCE and booked a round the world flight for two months. Without Melon!

Chapter 5

The end of the course came and Rob had passed. There was no graduation ceremony, this was reserved for the non-proper universities!

The day before he went away Rob was offered an English teacher job at a school in Coalville. He accepted it even though he had a History job in Norfolk!

Rob had asked Melon to marry him and she was flying out to meet him in Los Angeles in 2 months. Melon and Rob's Mam dropped him off at Heathrow and he was gone through into customs.

As the 747 sped down the runway and lifted off there was a huge, dull thud and Rob though that this was the end. But nothing happened. The flight to Mumbai was mostly Indians and the strange thing was that most of them brought their own food in stainless steel stacking bowls. The airline food on the British Airways flight was curry and Rob loved it.

Upon arriving in India Rob's senses were heightened with the noise of people, traffic. The smell of sewage and the assault of every kind of humanity passing by. He got into a taxi and asked to go to a central hotel. The scenes out of the window were amazing. Building being erected, sparks flying into the streets. Cars and motorbikes everywhere. Brightly painted Lorries with fancy pelmets and painted cows wandering through the city. All the signs were in English and there were London Double decker red busses. Rob had been all around the world and most countries emulated America. India looked like it wanted to be Britain.

The taxi driver took Rob to a door way in the Colaba district. It looked horrible but it led up to a first floor marble reception. Rob booked in for the week. He explored the local area, visiting the museum and the entrance price calculated to less than 1 pence in conversion.

He ate at a canteen on a corner underneath a cinema. Curry was served on metal plates with a naan bread but no cutlery. Rob observed the locals scooping up their food with their naans. Rob copied with a pieces of naan in both hands. The locals looked on in disgust. Rob later found out that Indians only ate with one hand as they wiped their backsides with the other.

Rob decided to go to the cinema that night as it was in English. Moulin Rouge starring Ewan Macgregor et al. It passed a couple of hours and as Rob was leaving the foyer a well-spoken Indian man introduced himself and politely asked Rob to join him at a bar for some conversation.

The pair walked down the crowded street and just as the man led Rob down an alleyway two street urchin boys who had constantly asked Rob for money approached. They looked concerned and said to Rob 'Mister. Misterr, he is a bad man, please don't go with him!'

The man's demeanour changed, he swore violently at the children and tried to grab and hit them. Rob walked off quickly in the other direction with the man shouting after him. Rob was pleased to reach Leopold's Café and have a cold beer.

The days in Mumbai were spent exploring the area. He went to the train terminal and gawped at its Victorian Gothic splendour and he visited the park where the dead were lain covered in peanut oil so that the horrible black Ravens picked at the bones before they made their final journey down the river.

He visited Chowpatty Beach that was strewn with litter and Rob was amazed by the homelessness. Some families living in disused Concrete pipes with satellite dishes on the top and electric cables running to the street lights like snakes. He would go for a stroll every night along the sea front past the Gateway of India, the Indian designed monument to George V in 1913.

It was running the gauntlet. He was constantly approached by hawkers. A man walked in stride with Rob he said 'Your toenails are a disgrace sir!'

Rob looked down at his Dolce and Gabbana sandals at then at the man who was dressed in rags and obviously homeless. A bit further along a man deftly and quickly stuck a metal rod in Rob's ear and pulled out ear wax and then offered to clean his ears. The man was like lightening.

It was a night flight from Mumbai to Singapore and Rob was upgraded to first class. He was in the upstairs section of the 747, it was like being in his own private plane. The food was served on porcelain and drinks from crystal glasses. He was awoken by the pilot welcoming the passengers to beautiful Singapore.

Rob found a cheap hotel next to Raffles and walked out into the early evening sunshine after a nap. He watched to expats and locals play touch rugby on a piece of colonial green in the city centre and walked to the bars and sat down with a Singha Beer. Some Jarheads had put Freefallin' on the jukebox and were singing loudly. Rob just sat minding his own business, enjoying his own company.

He noticed a group of ladies come in but did not think anything other than one looked just like Lady Diana. After a while Rob went to the bar and spoke to the ex-pat in the queue. He was a nice guy, friendly about Rob's age and worked for HSBC Bank in Singapore. Out of the blue the Lady Di' lookalike approached rob and asked if she could stay out with him because her friends were going home. Her friends checked on her and she bought a drink. Rob's ex pat friends eyebrows raised and looked at Rob with disbelief and admiration.

Rob and Lady Di' sat at a table and she asked how long Rob had lived in Singapore in her perfect posh English accent.
'Just one day and I leave for Sydney in two days'. He replied. It turned out that she had never been to England. She grew up in Kenya and attended ex pat schools and she was married to a Qantas airlines pilot. She took Rob to a club called Orchard Towers. It was in a high rise block and was full of Jarheads from the Mid-West and as thick as mince. As the night drew on Lady Di' and Rob headed outside and got a cab back to her house. It was a huge gated house and the entrance hall was all marble. The bed had black and cream silk sheets and they were cold as Rob slipped into them.
The bright sunlight awoken Rob and he wondered where the hell he was. He was piecing the night back together in his mind and the stranger slept soundly next to him. He didn't even know her name. By the side of Robs face was wet. It was thick brown sick. He had vomited in his sleep. He quickly got up and put his clothes on as he descended the spiral stairs. At the bottom there was a table with a picture of her and an older man with 2 children. Rob let himself out of the door and did a surfer run.

He flagged a taxi down and made for his hotel. He spent the whole day in bed with beer fear, but plucked up enough courage to go out at night to eat. He walked past the restaurants that had ducks hanging by their necks in the windows and mud crabs in tanks. He stopped at a restaurant by the water on a wharf and ordered Chicken skewers with a peanut dip. It was like Chicken Satay and came in a hotel fondue style cauldron. The following day he left Singapore for Sydney with Qantas.

As the flight approached Sydney, the airline played some sort of cheesy welcome home song! When he appeared from Customs his Aunty Betty was there with his Cousin's Son Bradley to meet him. His Aunt Betty reminded him of a skinnier, haggered version of his Mum. They arrived back in the Western Suburbs of Sydney and the bungalow was in a cul de sac like Neighbours. The contract from Coalville had arrived for Rob to sign and return and he did this.

It was to be two weeks of strange experiences. Bradley who was 14 would take Rob into Bradbury Town Centre. It was a little ugly sort of town that seemed to have a lot of deadbeats and homeless around. Rob and Brad would play rugby kicking at the posts on the field and his Aunt never cooked. Breakfast was MacDonald's, tea was KFC or Pizza.

Betty's husband worked nights as a security guard. A huge fat Irishman called Seamus. His brother in law lived next door he was a Belgian called Albert who was married to Seamus' Sister. Every Wednesday they went out, and they took Rob. They headed to a town called Liverpool and parked up. They took Rob up some stairs and into a room which had a sunken floor with seating and Greco styling.

Five women appeared and started speaking to the three men. Uncle Seamus had taken Rob to a House of ill repute! Later that day Seamus drove them to a club in a little village near Bradbury. There his mates were waiting. Big Jim was an ex Police detective who greeted Rob by saying' Who's got the pub now in Leicester?' He also accused Rob of wearing' Shelagh jeans'.

They drank Toohey's New in schooners which were three quarters of a pint. Rob was steaming drunk by 6 P.M. Betty came and picked them up. The next day they headed for Albert's holiday house at Ulladulla. It was a huge upside down house on the beach with balconies. It was like Home and Away. There was a yellow longboard in the garage and a body board. Rob and Brad spent the afternoon in the surf at Racecourse Beach. Lovely pristine turquoise water. A week earlier Brad had taken Rob surfing at Bondi. An awful place that was like Whitley Bay on a bad day. Australia came and went and Rob set off for Auckland with New Zealand Airways.

New Zealand is a funny place Rob felt that he was on the end of the world with the big skies. He spent a few days in Auckland, it was a city about the size of Hinckley! He wandered around and visited the museum, art gallery and Sky Tower. The architecture was a mix of colonial wooden slats and Victorian pseudo Gothic brick with Queen Victoria's image everywhere. He decided to hire a car and head north. He found a thermal swimming complex north of Auckland and went there one night. It was bliss and he sat in the hot outdoor baths watching Mean machine on the big screen. He carried on north to The Bay of Islands, through the countryside that reminded him of England in the 1950s. He went Whale and Dolphin spotting and was totally underwhelmed.

Next was Rotarua. It stunk of Sulphur. It was a town built upon thermal activity. He saw geysers and even the hotel had a thermal bath. The Maoris were a large race with many women sporting chin and mouth facial tattoos. He drank in the local pub which was an old Police station, built in the English 1950s brick style called the Pig and Whistle.

Rob landed in Honolulu and he had reserved a hotel room for the week in Waikiki. It was on Brewer's Street and it had a mirrored ceiling! Rob got there in the afternoon and made his way down to the beach. He watched the surf for an hour and returned to his room after buying some Slitz beer and clam chowder from a shop.

After a sleep Rob cooked his Chowder and sat on his balcony listening to The Charlatans on his mini disc player and drinking his beer. He had a few beers in Waikiki in the International Market Place and ended up in a club called Moose Mcgillycodys. The rest of the week was spent surfing the Waikiki reefs on a huge hire board. It was at least 13 feet long and 5 inches thick. It was so heavy that one day Rob was so tired he struggled and panicked paddling back in. Rob could not put sunscreen on his own back and so he had horrendous sunburn. He bought some painkilling spray and spent the next few days in a hire car visiting, Pearl Harbor [which ironically was full of Japanese tourists]. The North Shore and breaks like Haleiwa and Waimea. Rob surfed Haleiwa as it was small at 1-2 feet. A Puffa fish came to the surface as he paddled out through the country park and expanded itself in his face.

I woman stopped Rob in the street and asked him how George Harrison was? Like he should personally know him. It was the first time that Rob had been lonely on the trip and he looked forward to seeing Melon in Los Angeles tomorrow.

The night flight to LAX was with American Airlines and Rob noticed that the big chrome bird did not have life vests but used the seat cushions as a flotation aid. This unnerved him. When he landed in LAX, Melon was waiting for him and walked him back to the hotel where she was staying with her parents. She led him into the bathroom and bent over the sink!

They drove through the Mojave Desert to a hotel in Desert Springs. It was situated upon a golf course and in the shadow of Mount Jacinto. Joshua Trees were everywhere. The hotel was pure luxury and even had a boat and river inside of it. Pink Flamingos stood outside in the lake.

They had a laid back week. John and Rob hit balls on the range with scrawny Roadrunner birds lurking around. The food was great and Rob had the best steak ever in Palm Springs. Melon, John and Rob went horse riding on a ranch with a cowboy who looked like the weather beaten Marlborough man. The week soon drew to an end and they drove to Las Vegas through the desert.

They met Rob's Mam and her boyfriend, a bullish sort of man who rarely told the truth, from the flight that Rob had paid for. Rob's Mam cried when she saw her hotel room as it was much better than her house. Rob's Mam and her bloke loved Vegas. Rob paid for them to see Tom Jones at MGM and they had seat next to Tony Curtis.

It was the day before Rob and Melon's wedding and Rob, John and Henry went to hire Elvis jumpsuits. They walked out of The Jockey Club Hotel and onto the Strip and the traffic nearly stopped. Hooter's blared out and the three men. They could not walk for more than ten yards without being stopped for a photo. They went to an Elvis show and sat on the front row, stony faced. The impersonator double checked and forgot his lyrics. They didn't pay for a drink all night from Caesar's Palace to The Bellagio. They were absolutely steaming drunk and Rob slept on the bathroom floor spewing his Knob Creek all over the pan.
The wedding was at the Little Chapel of The West. Noel Gallagher was married there a week before. There were only 4 people at Rob's wedding and when they walked out some youths drove past and shouted out of the window 'You shouldn't have gone and done it Dude'.

Chapter 6

Back in Blighty and Melon and Rob had bought an 18th Century cottage in a tiny village near Ashby de la Zouch. It was time for Rob to begin teaching. So after two teacher training days of department meetings, schemes of work and pastoral meetings [which are a complete waste of time]. Rob had to plan his lessons and begin a new career.

On his first day he had a year 10 tutor group. Rob was nervous and reading his first register he called Christopher Grey, Christopher Gay. The Coalville High School stood upon a hill, made of local stone. It was surrounded by a mini Lake District and bracken and rocks.

It was for students from year 10 to 13 and was ran upon left wing, liberal lines. No school uniform, teachers could wear jeans and emphasis was upon academia and humanity. Within his first few lessons Rob realised some students could be a handful. One lad ran off from his lesson and Rob chased him down the corridor. Rob soon realised that this was not the 1980s.

Rob threw everything into his lessons, his character and linked it with the students experience as he dissected Romeo and Juliet and Steinbeck. The students responded and he got great results at the end of the year. He used praise culture and belief. Rob was even nominated for an award by his students that could have led to a Queen's award but it was far too soon. Rob's teaching was simple. Read section, apply to student's life experiences and write and quote. No need for the ridiculous bull of De Bono or Kagen. It's about interest, identify and validity. Nothing else. If it's worth nothing to you, then it's worth nothing. As Morrissey said 'It's about MY life'. Rob had 3 posters in his room. The Stone Roses, The Smiths, the Queen is Dead and New Order, Regret. All aimed to educate and the posters bought from the record store in the Leicester Fish Market!

His first half term was hard. Jenna a year 10 girl stood up in one lesson and said 'oooo my bum!' Rob said

'Jenna! Sit down and don't shout things like that out!'

She replied' Well I've burnt my bum on the radiator, see'. With that she turned around and pulled her jeans down revealing a Union Jack thong.

Rob was learning, he was in unfamiliar territory. A year 10 girl in his class approached him at the end of tutor time and asked for help. She asked for money for a taxi to Loughborough so that she could have an abortion. Rob did not know what to do. He gave her the money. He had no idea that it was safeguarding. He had not been given one single session on safeguarding. Perhaps it wasn't even a thing then? There were certainly no CBS or DBS checks. He did tell his head of department though, who just dismissed it with the words 'Silly girl'.
Rob soon became friends with Jock a young P.E teacher and part of Rob's English timetable soon became GCSE P.E. Rob began playing rugby again. He was recruited by the Head of French to play for Loughborough RFC. Rob had his first game in the second team against Syston RFC. Rob had always been plagued by the passing of time in his head and he was always shocked by it. For example seeing Terry Waterman as Minder then in the blink of an eye seeing the aged Waterman in New Tricks!

Rob used to see the County players and ex Tiger's players and struggle to compete. Now he was playing against them. Archer, Robin Nockles, Chris Tresler, et al. Rob scored four tries! He was by far the best player on the pitch! Prompted to the first XV the next week Rob decided to do the Great North Run instead. His first visit to Geordie land.

Jock was a character and often tutted at by the older staff. He was thought of as unprofessional but when Rob worked with him in P.E, Jock was ultra-professional and strict. But he did constantly do stupid things. On one occasion whilst Rob was teaching Volleyball in the gym, Jock who smoked went through the kid's coats in the changing rooms stealing their cigarettes.

Jock could be a loose cannon. If he disliked a kid he would often kick a ball at them, accidently, on purpose. One day he was walking up the school path to work with Rob and two year 11 boys walked past. One said 'Och aye Jocky'.

Jock kneed him in the groin in one motion and carried on walking, whilst the boy was doubled up. Jock was a young man and spent most of his weekends drunk in Oadby with his mates. He would come into work hungover and often sleep his free periods hidden away in the P.E store cupboard on the crash mats. He could be a bad influence for Rob as they would often go for a beer on Friday lunchtimes and before parents' evenings in the Forest Rock pub next door.

One parents' day the pair did not have any appointments for an hour so Jock talked Rob into going for a swim in the school swimming pool. Emma the Head of Sociology found them swimming naked with Radio 1 blaring out. 'You've got parents waiting!'

Rob was also tired on Monday mornings, he was absorbed by surfing. Melon and he had bought a 1966 Volkswagen Campervan and spent most weekends in Cornwall. Rob liked the Towan Beach Break and surfed mainly there and Perranporth. Melon was interested in witchcraft and made Rob stop frequently at the Witchcraft Museum in Boscastle.

It is here that she bought many things including a huge witchy ball that witches hang in their windows to ward off evil spirits. A lot of the witch craft things interested Rob as a Historian. The Hagg Stones to ward off the Devil and promote fertility. They were also used to stop the Devil from riding horses during the night. As Melon could not have children this was poignant.

Red candles for love, green for money and of course baubles. It's ironic that Melon was interested in baubles as this was a major source of production in Whitwick, where she was from in the 18th Century. One night Melon asked Rob to put her huge witchy ball up in the window of their ancient cottage. It was a late November day and already dark at 4-30 p.m. Their cottage was over 3 floors and in the attic they once found an early Victorian Child's shoe, another old custom or witchcraft. Rob was screwing the bauble into the window plinth and Melon tapped him hard upon the shoulder. He turned around as the tap was so firm he thought that she must have not liked his Do It Yourself skills.

Rob turned around and there was no one there. This was one of many strange occurrences in the old cottage. The witchy ball worked by gathering dust and the process of wiping it clean, cleaned the evil spirits away.

Rob knew from the very beginning that Melon could not have children. During that summer they tried twice for IVF but failed. It was not just the ten grand that was lost, something sadder was lost in their relationship and hope seemed to have gone. Ebbed away like an outgoing tide. It was unclear if this tide was going to return as strong. Melon's parents sensed the couple's pain and showered them with money. A holiday to Kuala Lumpur and Hawaii for Christmas. They bought Rob a Porsche 944 and a Karmann Convertible. Rob was not ungrateful he was just hurting and now he felt bought.

The second year of teaching for Rob was teaching Humanities rather than English. He wished he's never changed. He loved teaching English and his department were insular and protective of him. The Humanities Department was big and fragmented. It would to be wrong to say that there was any rivalry or professional jealousy at the school. Holdsworthy, the Head teacher was liberal and cared about his staff. The senior leadership team sat with the staff at lunch and break time and the staffroom was busy. There was no divide between the SLT and staff. Rob didn't realise it at the time but these were the Last Days of the Raj, the last halcyon days of teaching, where teachers were treated like professionals and not call centre corporate kids.

The new term started and Rob settled into his new faculty. He soon realised that English taught about the human condition not Humanities. The way History and Geography was taught was dull and mechanical. Focussing upon skills that don't really exist and missing the whole point of the story. A missed opportunity.

Rob's rugby team was excelling and was unbeaten by anyone in the county. He raised the money for the kit and for the posts. The school was bottom of the league tables academically and had no money. After every game Rob would get the students to steal the posher, other school's equipment.
Redistribution of wealth, Rob called it. They happily stole everything from javelins to rugby balls and all in-between.
Rob went on two trips this academic year. One to Rome with the design faculty, where he had to share a double bed with the head teacher and another to London. Rob had embarked upon a Master's degree in English Local History. It was a time when working in education meant that it was lifelong learning and teachers were encouraged to progress academically: not CPD bull: not pedagogy bull, plenaries and starters, marginal gains, but real academic knowledge.
Andy Reeve was the Head of Humanities and the scheme of work included using films like East is East and the analysing them and apply the learnt knowledge, this was something that Rob was going to use as a tool for the rest of his career and it was sometimes frowned upon.

Rob had read the work of Southin at University and how it was the opposite of what's thought of woodland folk and isolated communities. They are actually immigration and emigration centres. So when Rob took part in a visit to London he was totally unaware that a great deal of his year 10 students had never been past Leicester let alone London. The visit to the Imperial War Museum and then central London went without a hitch until the train journey home.
'Sir, Bethel, has a pigeon up his coat'.
'Eh what Saddington?' was Rob's reply and Saddington repeated himself. Rob approached Bethel who had a Lacoste blue zip up blouson jacket on.
'Lee have you got a pigeon up ya coat?' Bethel shook his head. 'C'mon Lee unzip your jacket'.
With that Bethel unzipped his coat a little and a pigeon popped its head out.
'Bloomin' heck Lee where did you get that from? Where are you going to keep it?'
Saddington replied for Bethel 'He got it from Trafalgar Square Sir, he's going to keep it in a cardboard box in his shed as a pet'.

Rob eventually got Bethel to hand him the bird. Realeasing it then became a problem. However when the train stopped at some points Rob undid the door window and threw the bird free. Thud! It bird was hit by a speeding train going past in the opposite direction!

Another ill-fated excursion was Jock's white-water rafting trip to Holme Pierrepoint in Nottingham. Rob, Jock and 10 students climbed aboard a raft with an instructor. They paddled through the rapids and then the boat shot up in the air and everyone bar the instructor was in the swirling and churning freezing cold water. Rob popped up underneath the boat in complete darkness. By the time he had got back into the boat they were fishing crying students out of the water, except one. Jeffers had been washed right through the rapids and out into the River Trent. When he was reused he was in shock and had messed himself.

In his second year a new teacher joined the school. A blonde surfish looking design teacher, Ade. They became good friends and now most weekends were spent with Ade and his mates Bobby [a designer for Sone Island] and Barry a film director. They surfed Devon, staying in Croyde and surfing the beautiful green waters of Puttsborough and the great longboard break of Saunton Sands.

Things were getting really strained with Melon and even a dream holiday to Australia, visiting Sydney, Brisbane and a night in the desert at Uluru could not stop the rot. The seams were splitting apart. One day Rob decided to leave he was going to get up early and just go to Cornwall and go on supply. He set his alarm for 5am and had a restless night's sleep. He opened his eyes and wondered what would happen if the electric went off and he missed his alarm. He started at the red digits that read 2; 49. Then they faded into black. He got up. The lights in the house did not work. The electric had gone off. He went into the street, the street lights were still on. He checked the circuit board that had not tripped. Rob went back to bed and the clock was back on. He decided not to go.

The summer came and went and it was Rob's third year. He decided to move back in with his mother in Leicester and left Melon. After a few weeks there was a school night out. Rob was drunk and ended up snogging the young French teacher and making out with a knee trembler in the St Margaret's underpass. Rob saw her a few more times but back at work she was telling staff and students that they were going out. Rob didn't like this so he called it all off. She went on the sick for a month with stress!

Rob had moved back in with Melon and they were trying to work through their barren relationship. It was a mistake and Rob made lots of them in this period. His Porsche battery was flat so he charged it up overnight. The next morning he put the battery back into the car and started the engine. He got 20 yards up the lane before the car stopped and was full of acrid smoke. He had not put the battery in the tray correctly and the terminals had arced across the bonnet burning the electrics out!

The French teacher returned to work and asked if she could have a word with Rob by the photocopier. Rob smiled and agreed. She said 'I've just come back from the doctor's and I have Chlamydia'.

Rob went home and told Melon the lot, she punched him in the face. It actually hurt Rob. They both took the day off and attended Clinic Six at Leicester Royal Infirmary. One had to take a butcher's counter style ticket and wait to be seen. Rob in his suit and the other customer's absolute scruffs. The investigation was completed for everything and Rob had not got any diseases.

He returned to work and said to the French teacher 'Can I have a word? I've been to the clinic and been tested and I have nothing'. She replied 'That's funny neither have I'.

In the May Rob went on a Benidorm trip with Steve and the Red Cow lads. At the airport Rob thought that he'd better call in sick over the phone so he rang the school answer machine. Just as he was saying his name and how he had an upset stomach the tannoy came on and said 'Britannia flight bn231 please board through gate 27'. Upon returning to work Kath the receptionist just smiled at Rob.

During that trip Rob spent the whole four days with a girl from Leeds. She cried on the day he left and kept on calling him when he was home. Louise was good to him on the trip. Rob was going through a bad time and took 3 E's that he bought off a guy in the square. Louise took Rob to the beach. He was out of his gourd and didn't know where he was. She just sat with him, giving him water and saying 'I wish that you were normal again'.

The good thing about the trip was that Rob was with his old friends including Hewitt. Dave Hewitt slept with an eye mask on. One night when he was asleep Steve shoved a Twix chocolate bar finger up his bottom. Rob and Steve were amazed, Dave's bottom sucked the finger in and up!

Upon his return to England things were really fraught with Melon. Rob spent most of his time drinking Brandy and Coke and listening to Gene through his headphones. Drink had been a big thing to Rob, he drank to cope with the stresses of teaching and his relationship. They tried to carry on as normal. They went to see Gene in Nottingham Rescue Rooms and they were fantastic, energetic and inspiring. They saw them again a month later supporting Morrissey at Mo fest on the South Bank in London and had a nice weekend in Greenwich. But it was the death rattle of the relationship really.

Rob had got himself a new job as Assistant Head of the Humanities Faculty in a school on a large council estate to the east of Leicester City Centre and only had a month before the summer holidays. Bizarrely enough the French teacher asked Rob for a drink and like an idiot he went. That night he ended up rattling her upon the bonnet of his car down a country lane under the stars at Shaker stone. A week later , the French aural exams were being held in the old house at school, which was a separate building that used to be the caretaker's house. Rob was given a cover lesson as the person who sat with the student before the exam.

Madame Bear was the French teacher taking the exam. The student did not turn up. The next thing Rob knew she was leaning over her desk and itching up her skirt revealing her lacy French underwear. Rob was back scuttling her within minutes! A few days later she turned up at his upstairs room 4. The door was locked and more work place back scuttling!

Rob was pleased that he was leaving especially when Jock sat next to him in the staffroom. Jock said 'What did you do last night mate? I went out with Leigh'.

'Who's Leigh?' Rob replied

'Leigh Summers in Year 12'.

'Blooming' eck mate. Don't tell me that, I don't want to know', and Rob cut him dead. It was the end of the conversation.

A few weeks later Jock spoke to Rob again. 'You'll never believe it mate, Leigh's pregnant'.

Rob had no choice but to tell his line manager.

The school holidays came and the gorgeous hippy art technician, Mandy had given Rob her number. Rob left Coalville and the next day he was at Ruda campsite in Croyde for a week's surfing with Ade. On his way back he kept on getting messages from Melon asking what time he was home. Upon arriving home, she was waiting and told him that she had left him. It was the right thing to do. She drove away in her Ford KA and Rob entered the cottage, everything had gone. He got into his car and drove to Sennen Cove to surf.

Upon his return Rob went out for a drink into Ashby with Mandy and at the end of the night he found himself on her sofa taking off her white thong to reveal a full bush.

If a house had synergy then Rob's cottage did. There were scratching noises between the walls and floors at night and one morning Rob went to put his shoes on and they were full to the brim of cat biscuits. He did not have a cat!

Rob was bored so he contacted Madame Bear and they booked a trip to Iceland. At Heathrow Airport they boarded the Icelandair flight to Iceland and sat behind Bjork! The visit went well, catching a bus from the airport to the hotel was a pain but Reykjavik was tiny. Rows of weather boarded colourful houses. The couple went whale watching and visited the Blue Lagoon thermal baths. The dirty French Madame of course pulled her bikini bottoms to the side in the pools.

By the end of the trip she was annoying the hell out of Rob. She was so boring all she spoke about was her family, how her Dad sang Rocky Raccoon outside the Old Salutation pub in Sennen and how he did mathematical calculations to do the lottery. Rob could scream at times.

Upon his return Rob was pleased to be going to Newcastle for the weekend on a stag night with Hewitt. Dave picked him up from Markfield Services at 9AM on the Saturday morning in his new Audi A4. They got to Whitley Bay about 2PM and found a hotel. It was one street of bars and Dave parked his car a few streets away as he didn't like the look of the area. Whilst the stag group went out to see the strippers in the Whitley Bars, Dave and Rob went to Jesmond to have a club sandwich lunch in a bar much more them.

It was early evening by the time they returned and they looked out of the window to see the carnage developing in the street. Rob thought that the only way he was going to get through this was by getting drunk so he thought that he'd just drink Stella. It turned out to be an alright evening. They started off in the Fire Station and worked their way down the strip to the bottom and a bar called Pier 21. Vickers had just reappeared into the pub bragging that he had just taken a girl out to the beach and shot his onions all over her back, he had sand all over the knees of his jeans. It was a bar where you stuck to the floor and your sleeve's stuck to the bar too. The lads were amazed by the raised island that the local sorts got up and danced like they were in a P Diddy video. The last port of call was the nightclub Deep, and that's where Rob's life was to change again.

Chapter 7

It was a pretty soulless sort of club, full of early twenties and younger and the music was rank, meaningless R and B. Rob thought about jacking it in and going back to the hotel. He was bored. Just as the kebab was calling, a girl nearly burnt him with her cigarette.
'Whooo easy Tiger' was Rob's cry as he dusted ash off his black Valentino shirt.
The girl just sniggered, she had a big moon face and blonde hair. She pointed at Rob's shoes and sniggered. 'Ha ha, white shoes!'
'Get lost, these shoes are Dolce and Gabana I bought them in Rome'. Rob retorted.
'Where are you from anyways?'
Moon face replied 'My name's Arabella and I live in Heaton'.
'Eaton? Near Slough?' Rob replied
She was confused. She asked for Rob's number as Hewitt wanted to go and Rob gave it to her not expecting a reply as it was 300 miles to Leicester. He wasn't attracted to her anyways.
The next day after a Macdonald's breakfast near York, Rob's phone pinged a text alert. It was her, asking how he was and that she was hungover. She asked if she could ring him about 6pm at night and Rob agreed.

6 P.M came and his phone rang. She told him how she'd like to meet up and she didn't mind long distance relationships as her brother had one between California and Huddersfield. She asked him to visit her the next weekend. Rob had nothing to do so agreed.

Rob decided to drive up, his Mam and mates thought that he was mad. But he did it anyway. She took him to Longsands Beach and Rob did not realise that you could surf up in Newcastle. The area was beautiful and he had a great time. He was soon going up every weekend.

Rob's new job was going well. Whilst it was a challenging area Rob was greeted by the kids as one of their own. It could have been because of his Leicester accent or because he had gone to the football as a hooligan with some of their fathers, he will never know but he had no behavioural problems. Rob kept himself to himself and he was ultra-professional. He was earning really good money. The days were long and he got home to the spooky, dark empty cottage. He'd become exclusive to Arabella with the exception of the school Christmas party where he had lips on with the Asian IT teacher Dee and the young Geography teacher.

Rob went to Hawaii for Christmas with his Mam and Henry. He was marking R.E mock papers on the plane. They had a one night stopover in Atlanta. They got there about 2pm and it was already getting dark. After settling in to the hotel they decided to go downtown. They headed for the MARTA underground and failed at the first hurdle, the turnstile. A black guy with his jeans on back to front, large woolly hat and oversized puffa coat approached them. Rob thought to himself 'Here we go'.

To his embarrassed surprise the guy offered his help and money and paid for the three of them to get through the turnstile. In downtown Atlanta they were only white people that they see. Of course Rob thought, because of the slave trade and he began to think of the horrors and how a whole people were transported half way across the world and are now in the majority. But seek no revenge.

Rob bought a Pepsi even though it's the birthplace of Coca Cola. They went for dinner at a sport's bar near the hotel and Rob had the best chicken wings he'd every had and they watched Atlanta play football on the big screens.

Hawaii was amazing at Christmas. Waikiki was full of light. All the flats had fairy lights on and the Moana Shopping Centre had a flip flop wearing Santa riding a Dolphin. Rob surfed Waikiki every day and Christmas lunch was eaten in Duke's Canoe Club on the beach. The whole city was magical and winked and glistened at night. The bath that Rob surfed in gave up gently crumbling turquoise waves. The ice cold and rich eggnog milkshakes from Wendy's were addictive. Some people thought that Rob was gay going on holiday with his parents especially with his David Beckham hair and clothing. The flight back was via Salt Lake City and the freezing cold Plain's landscape amazed Rob as much as the Mormon locals. The only sad thing about the trip was that Rob's Mam developed a cough that would not go away.

Back in the U.K Rob's life was for another change. He visited Arabella when he got home and surfed Longsand's Beach. Rob caught a clean large left handed wave near the rip tide and pool. He was hooked, he was definitely going to move north and applied for every North East job in the Times Educational Supplement.

Rob accepted an Easter start at a Pupil Referral Unit in South Shields teaching English. / His school in Leicester were gutted and he was approached by the head and Deputy asking if there's anything that they could offer him to stay? They did not want to lose teachers of his quality apparently. Rob had sold his cottage for 3 times what he had paid for it and moved in with Arabella with over a hundred and thirty grand in his bank.

Chapter 8

The move went well and Rob moved to Newcastle. He managed to get all of his belongings into one van. Rob was not attracted to Arabella but she made him laugh and she surfed.
Rob's new job was in an old part of South Shields. A dreary Victorian, forgotten sort of a place, right out of Catherine Cookson called Tyne Dock. The unit was an old disused primary school that was run down. There were 3 main classrooms, English, Maths and Science. He knew it was dodgy when the head of service invited him to lunch on the last day before the Easter Term and the previous incumbent was there trying to have his leaving do. Awkward.

Each class had 7 to 10 pupils who had been rejected from schools for behavioural problems. They were year 7 to 9 and some were dangerous or vulnerable. It was like the film Scum, the kids fought to prove their worth and disrupted where they could. All the teachers had to be trained in a control and restraint course called Team-teach.

Rob found it barbaric and treated the students like people and how he would like to be taught and he had very few problems.

However, some of the other teachers hated the kids and tables and chairs would fly across the classrooms every lesson.

In one lesson a student bursted into Rob classroom. 'Help. Help Sir, Lee Coffee's gan mad!'

Rob rushed into the Maths lesson and Coffee had another student in a head lock and was repeatedly stabbing him in the back of the neck with a biro. Rob had to wrestle him off and covered in blood escorted him out of the classroom. Coffee escaped over the school fence.

Rob wanted a proper secondary school job and began applying. Every weekend was spent surfing from Bamburgh down to Saltburn and the couple also went away in Rob's campervan. The Sand Dancer culture intrigued Rob and he had his first Savaloy Dip and Ham and Pease Pudding Stottie. The Geordies really did say Wye Aye and the Sand Dancers said Aye Why Aye. The couple booked a cottage in Croyde for their summer holidays but in the meantime they bought a huge Edwardian House on Brown's Bay in Cullercoats with Rob putting most of his cash into it.

The week before the jobs deadline Rob got a job as Head of Humanities at a school in Ashington. He was over joyed. The teachers in his Pupil Referral Unit, told Rob not to do it as it was a hell hole. Surely it couldn't be worse than a PRU?

Ashington was once one of Britain's main mining towns. It had many pits and a plethora of sporting stars such as the Milburns, and the Charltons. Thatcher beat the life out of the miners and the town in the 80s and being isolated in Northumberland about 15 miles north of Newcastle it has never properly recovered to its once proud past. No infrastructure or industry was provided to the area after the loss of mining and alongside towns like Blyth it was a tragedy. There is no comparison in Leicestershire where near full employment exists in middle and multi-cultural England.

Rob went into his new school over the summer and it was chaos. The previous Heads of History and R.E had left in huff and just dumped everything, book and all in one room in bin liners. They had deleted all resources and schemes of work off the system and mixed the Specification booklets up so Rob had to work to even find out what courses were being taught.

To confound matters all of Rob's faculty bar two were Newly Qualified Teachers. The term started and Rob worked every hour he could, planning, resourcing and coaching. His team were responsive and he forged a good unit with them and they all bought into Rob's ethos and did their best.

It was obvious that the school was going through a transition. There was a new head teacher and senior leadership team and over half of the long serving previous task had left with those who hadn't being disgruntled. There had been a student's strike a few months before where students had walked out of the school and set up a picket line outside the gates in protest of the new head Mrs Lesley. The new head's response was to conduct a witch hunt being paranoid that the staff had organised it. She also became super liberal with the students who now wore their own clothes and ruled the school without recourse. However, she was not so lenient with her staff.

Rob had never heard the word capability in his 4 or 5 years teaching. He thought that teaching was for life. Now the Head bantered it around as if it was a way of getting rid of who she didn't want. Rob shared his concerns with Sarah, the new Head of English.

Rob was fair with his staff, he protected them and wanted them to do well in their careers. They worked hard and Rob went out with them a lot into Newcastle at weekends drinking in North Bar near the Station. Rob recognised the DJ from surfing Tynemouth, a lad called Titch.

Arabella and Rob saw lots of bands in Newcastle including Ian Brown where the gig was so boisterous that the concert had to be emergency emptied because there was fear of the floor collapsing. The pair went to Glastonbury in Rob's camper and she was in her element. She said Rob had 'showed her how to live her life'. It was Rob's second time at Glastonbury, the first was backstage with Plasticman, a DJ that his friend Martyn knew from University.

Work was stressful. The behaviour was really bad and at times reached the same levels as the Pupil Referral Unit. Rob had some lovely classes and between him and his NQT Francis, got reasonable results at GCSE and A/Level over the next three years. There was another History teacher called Jacqui and she was middle aged and a mess. She's go on huge benders with her new bloke and pop out at lunch and break time to snog him in his car.

One day in December she just disappeared. In January the head asked Rob and the Assistant Head teacher to go around her house in the afternoon. They got to Jacqui's house in Cramlington, the bins were overflowing with Stella cans and the curtains were drawn but there were more beer cans upon the window sill. They knocked on the door, no reply but the door was open, they peered into the darkness and shouted. All did not seem well so they called the Police.

A Police car arrived and the situation was explained. The copper got Rob to put plastic bags on his feet and they entered the property with the Policeman's torch and him shouting out into the darkness. 'All of a sudden the naked Jacqui appeared at the top of the stairs 'Get out of my house'! Rob never saw her again.

They employed a middle aged guy on long term cover. Bob was a bit odd. One day he walked past Rob's room with a box that was chirping. Rob went into his room. 'What's in the cardboard box mate?'

'Chicks for James Bradley in year 9'.

'Bob you can't keep them in your roommate, you'll have to put them back into your car'. Bob replied 'I came on the buses.

There were a few animal incidents at the school. Every now and then a dog would somehow get into the school [usually a Staffy] and cause mayhem. Rob had not seen this since he was at school in New Parks and Mark Vickers's Grandpa stabbed Andy Lake's dog with his umbrella when it went onto the rugby pitch.

Occasionally, The Head also brought her dog into School and the Christmas service at the local church was attended by a random dog and a man chasing it with a falcon on his wrist. It was a whole new world to Rob. For some reason the kids from Lynemouth and Newbiggin often had horses and Rob past them sometimes in their horse and traps on the Spine Road. One day a year 9 student was late for Rob's afternoon lesson and when he queried her tardiness she replied 'Sorry I'm late Sir, but I've been willicking at Cresswell with my Nan.'

This meant that her Grandmother had taken her to pick Winkle shell fish at Cresswell Bay. The language confused Rob. In his first lessons a student said 'How Sir, can I gan to the toilet how?' How was used as a word to say excuse me or to get attention.

Another student asked him if 'he had a durg?' A dog. There were lots of new words, Yherm meaning home, gan for go, chebble for table, forky tail for earwig and spoaching for looking. Roley the P.E teacher was from Wooler and he actually rolled his R's.
The school was so out of control and turmoil. A lot of it caused by the huge changes in management and staff. Rob thought that if he ever had to take a role in which there were previous and long standing staff, he would change things gradually after standing back and analysing what worked and what needed tweaking. This common sense would lead to the end of Rob's career.

Rob encountered another type of youth. The Charva. They wore Berghaus Mirapeak coats, had tracksuit bottoms tucked into socks and Nike TN air trainers and caps. Their caps were worn at a 45 degree handle. The sometimes rode tiny bikes and spoke with a droning drawl. They all listened to a music called New Monkey, which was a kind of shouting, toasting, rapping music. Very white, often racist and mentioned drugs. New Monkey was a club in South Shields. Roley had this double period for year 11 on Wednesday afternoons called Recreation. All it entailed was the Chavs playing New Monkey and Pool whilst the good kids from North Seaton revised or played 5 a side.

The new Senior Leadership were keen to use Rob's optimism and professionalism. They wanted rid of the Head of Science so they paired rob up with him to get evidence. Rob was not like that and actually thought that the Head of Science was a good teacher and rather than furthering his own position he sent a glowing report to protect him. The kids were horrible in Science and actually wrote Ratty's Lab above his door.

Rob was also asked to be Head of 6th Form but he could not bring himself to oust the present Head of Sixth Form from her job. Eventually he succumbed and became associate senior leadership shadowing the new deputy head with timetabling.

The previous deputy had employed Rob. Mr Paul Ray was good to Rob but Machiavellian. He tried to get Rob to find out information and he wanted rid of the other deputy. Rob's progress at work was soon to come to a halt. One night after school Mr Ray had asked Rob to do something. Rob texted Francis on his way home 'Fat Paul's a dodgy devil'. Rob was not feeling bad for himself but ashamed that he had betrayed Mr Ray.

His phone went beep, beep and Rob checked his text. It was from Mr Paul Ray. It just said 'What?' Rob pulled over into the Silverlink car park and put his head into his hands.

The school was crazy. Rob took a Year 9 football team to Amble. The Chavs refused to play unless they wore their tracksuit bottoms tucked in socks or taken their East 17 style woolly hats off.

Rob and Arabella went away a lot. They made frequent visits to see her family in San Diego and stayed with them in beautiful La Jolla or Mission Hills. They surfed La Jolla a lot and Rob bought Arabella a thousand Dollar board from Surf Diva, she loved it and rode it well. They surfed Oceanside with its strange Marine's camp and met Jack Curran in the surf shop in the town and sank a few Sierra Nevada beers.

They went to India and in Delhi Rob was amazed how many people just slept on the streets. The hotel was good and as the sun came down every night Rob saw a thousand homemade kites flying across the huge city as he ate his ridiculously hot curry in the roof top restaurant.

Arabella was just stared at with her blonde hair by the locals and the couple booked a taxi to Agra. On the way they pulled up at some road works. As with any junction there were beggars and hawkers. Rob looked out of his window and a man was playing a flute and a Cobra was swaying about out of the top of a basket. In an instant the Cobra struck and bit the monkey sitting next to the man. The monkey just turned its head and scornfully sneered and rolled its eyes at the monkey on the chain.

Rob was disappointed with the empty structure of the Taj Mahal and actually thought that it was over rated. The next stop was Bangkok, which is always good and an assault on the senses, before heading off to Australia, where they stayed and surfed manly before moving off to Ulladulla and seeing hundreds of dolphins playing in the waves at Racecourse Beach. They stayed with Bella's friends in Canberra.

Rob hated Canberra. It was cold and reminded him of Cramlington, Soulless. Were huge celebrationary staues everywhere. Full of roundabouts and life behind high wooden fences. Just like Cramlington no one was around. Rob felt like Charlton Heston as the last man after an apocolypse. However, the one good thing is that one can stand on top of the politicians on the roof of Parliament.

A quick visit to New Zealand then Fiji. When they landed in Fiji they were greeted in the tiny airport by locals playing ukuleles and signing welcome giving out leis. The taxi bus drove through the darkness, along the roads past the small huts and open fires to Nandi where they were staying. The sea was full of sea cucumbers which were like 4 feet long snakes and the island was surrounded by a barrier reef.

The couple took a boat to Cloud break and an isolated atoll. They snorkelled in the crystal clear seas which were full of life but fell off really deep away from the reef. Back on dry land they were told that the Fijian's only stopped being cannibals a hundred years ago. Rob bought an antique flesh fork!

The strange cava ceremony consisted of a muddy bowl of root based water which had stimulants and clapping three times and shouting Bula before you drank the muddy liquid. Rob preferred a Bloody Mary.

Back at school Rob began to play rugby for John Leithead the exams officer who used to be a P.E Teacher. He placed for Morpeth RFC. Huge games against Alnwick where Rob made a try saving tackle to win and against Carlisle where Rob made tackle after tackle. Rob then had another season with Whitley Bay Rockcliff and made some good friends despite being sent off in his first game against Percy Park RFC. He'd immersed himself in Geordie life.

The head wanted rid of Leithhead's mate, the Head of P.E Roley. There were some members of staff that had been there years and were respected by generations. Rather than utilising these, the new guard wanted the old guard out. Mr Mordue was an excellent practioner. He was a silver fox and when he walked into the room the kids would be in absolute silence out of respect. He should have been made into senior leadership by the new guard and it would have solved lots of problems.

Roley was a slightly different kettle of fish. He had a heart of gold and was very much an organiser, so much so it could at times be the Roley Show. He was an excellent teacher but hated by the new guard and Roley made a huge mistake by organising the end of year party and inviting the previous head teacher to make a speech. Roley had a long history in the area and he was even the team manager for the Northumberland *It's a Knock out* team. Roley was banned from organising the end of year parties at Ashington Rugby Club, but he still did an unofficial one there that was attended by most staff, whilst the official one was attended by few. More fuel on his flames. They could not get Roley on capability so the way that they destroyed him was by promoting a member of his team to be his boss by making them SLT.

The Head teacher rewarded loyalty rather than ability and whilst Rob could not adhere to this ethos, there were many that would accept the Shilling. I suppose even Jesus had a price. The leadership team was added to with some teachers that shouldn't have been. However, these moved on in time to other leadership teams in other schools so Rob's perceptions could be jaundiced.

The school was a tough gig not just with its management but also with some of its students and families. On such students father had punched a horse at a Newcastle v Sunderland match. When Rob rang him up to complain about his son, who was a student it went straight to answerphone.
'Hello this is Mr Broon, leave a message and I'll get back to you unless you're the school then you can Fuck off'.

Chapter 9.

Rob had no chemistry with Arabella but he agreed to get married to her at the Grand Hotel in Tynemouth in June 2008. He thought this was his last chance of happiness.
Bizarre things happened at work before that and it didn't even compute with Rob's addled brain. The Christmas Party was held at a comedy club in Newcastle. After the turns Rob was at the bar. The posh French teacher approached him and said 'I can see it in your eyes that you are up for fun and my husband and I have an open relationship'.

Rob thought how odd and in the nick of time his friend approached the couple. However, over the Christmas Holidays the seed had been planted and was growing in Rob's brain, so the first day back after school he went to her office to see her. Within minutes she was pulling the back of his hair and he had her blouse and bra off!

A couple of months later Rob went on Roley's sixth form trip to Ford Castle for the weekend. It was organised like clockwork with treasure hunts to Holy Island and walks from Coldingham Bay in the Borders. That night drink flowed with the teachers and as Rob went to bed, the assistant head of sixth form grabbed him and pulled him into the toilet to try and snog him!

The next night he stood outside talking with Francis and she told Rob that she loved him! Rob went home for some peace and a surf.

It was now May and Arabella and Rob went to see The Complete Stone Roses at Newcastle Academy. A young female teacher from Rob's school approached them and said 'Hello'.

Arabella said 'She's good looking'. Rob shrugged it off, he'd never noticed her before. This was the most important chance meeting of his life. The young female teacher came to see Rob on Monday. She taught Biology and was beautiful with almond shaped eyes and a slight gap in her teeth. Over the next month they spent more and more time chatting at work and Rob knew he had to be with her. But he was getting married in a few days and he's just bought another huge Edwardian house in Cullercoats that had engulfed all of his capital.

The term ended and Rob got married. He rang the girl with the almond eyes on his wedding day and she was in tears. He went on his honeymoon and he sat in the hotel in the Florida Keys looking out of the window onto the pristine beach. There was a thunder storm and he watched a huge light green monitor type lizard run up a Palm tree. He went for a walk in the rain on his own. The hotel grounds were silent. He passed a small inlet from the ocean and there was a hotel employee feeding 3 wild manatees with cabbage. She handed one to Rob who joined in feeding the dinosaurs. It was a welcome break from his thoughts, from himself. He made a decision, he had to be with Almond eyes and he walked back to the room and told Arabella.

Chapter 10

One of the few things in life that one can be sure of is change. The key is how resilient one is and how one copes and welcomes change. Back in England it was change, change, and change for Rob.

He moved out and moved in with his Bouncer mate on St Peter's Basin in Newcastle. They both had Lambrettas and they became like an old married gay couple. Sunday dinners together and pints in the Bascule Pub. Quizzing each other about what time they got in at nights and washing their clothes with dishwasher tablets by mistake.

There were huge changes at school. Rob's school had been taken over and sold to the Church. It was now a multi- age academy from nursery through to year 13. A mass clear out again, the head lost her job and the senior leadership seemed to be filled by every aspiring middle leader in the area. The new super head was from London on a six figure salary and flew up on a Sunday and home on a Friday. Rob kept his post. The reasons that councils are keen to make school's academies is purely financial. The buildings, staff, resources are all a huge strain on a council and they are keen to jettison them. Huge academy chains were set up, private companies trying to make a buck. Corporate madness.

Things changed and a new school was built. The Queen and prince Phillip visited. Rob got the chance to meet Phillip and he was tiny and frail. The Prince shook Rob's hand gingerly and asked him 'I say, young man how many children are at this establishment?'

Rob replied 'there will be about 2500, Sir'.

'How dreadful', was Phillip's reply.

It became a witch hunt and getting rid of the old staff. Things had gone full circle for Rob and the pressure was on him. Every holiday was wasted worrying about results or observations. Every lesson was observed by the senior team and graded with an i-pad and the middle leaders had to answer for it every week with their line manager.

The stress was amazing, but the results actually went down. Five more years Rob went through this regime. Every summer in Mimizan or Biarritz or Portugal being miserable and dwelling and worrying about results. It was so unfair on his young family. Depression, weight gain, alcohol ass a by-product of the greedy bullies. The capability word was bounded around again and staff just disappeared. Some on gardening leave. Blame culture, fear of losing high salaries, poor leaders, it was in a spiral of change and blame.

Rob managed to get a new job in Gateshead but he still had two terms to work. He had booked to go to Glastonbury so he rang in sick. When he was in the bar in departures at Newcastle Airport at 10;30 in the morning, the Head teacher walked in and stared Rob straight into the eyes. On the Monday Morning Rob thought that he'd get called into the office, but nothing was said.

A few months later Rob went on a surf trip to Morocco with his mates. He called in sick for the week! When he got back to work the students all commented on Rob's tan.

He was called into the office and the deputy head said 'Robert a member of staff saw you last week in the Metro Centre and should have been at work'.

Rob couldn't say this but he felt like saying 'He must have good eye sight because I was in Bastard Africa in fucking Agadir you thick copper!'

Chapter 11

Rob had become a part of the Tyneside surf scene. He surfed every swell and felt guilty if he did not. There was no fear of bumping into Arabella, she was long gone moving out of the North East with the proceeds of the house sale. Rob lost £170,000 plus another £20,000 on his credit card to get out of the sham marriage five years previously.

Rob began hanging around with Baha, a shaper from The Bahamas who now lived in Tynemouth. Baha was out there with his shapes and his surfing. Rob surfed some odd places with him. They surfed Snab Point in Lynemouth, a reef break under the lee of the power station and climbing down a muddy bank past gypsy horses.

Rob went to the European Fish Fry with Baha. Rob flew with his board from Edinburgh to Shannon, whilst Baha drove there in his VW T4. They met up at Doombeg and surfed there before heading to La Hinch with the other Shapers. They parked up at the beach at night and shared a Red Wine and French dried sausage with Alex a French surfer from Bordeaux. Rob slept in his board bag in his hire van whilst Baha slept in his T4. Rob needed to go to the toilet in the night and had a poo on the beach. He was awoken at first light by a dog walker and his dog was gobbling up his poo. It couldn't get enough of it. This was the second time that this had happened. Rob once had a surf at Seaton Sluice and had to have a poo in the sand dunes. Malcolm Macdonald the bandy legged ex footballer and Toon legend came around the corner and his dog too ate Rob's poo. He should have marketed it.

The surf at La Hinch was canny and Rob surfed well on his big fish but it was soon time to go home, well after a few more pints of the black stuff.

They surfed the beautiful Sugar Sands. The picturesque Alnmouth , with its rips and Cresswell Bay. Rob shaped his own longboard in Baha's shaping room and did it back to front as a mad Baha experiment. Stu the Bear was horrified.

Stu the Bear was a grizzly old surfer in his 60s who repaired all the Tynemouth boards. He shaped too. He did not suffer fools gladly and he was not to be dropped in on or upset in the sea. Rob was lucky that Stu liked him. Stu was really good to Rob and always fixed his boards. He always fussed Rob's newly born son Nu and Stu always had time to talk and laugh with Rob. He was a generous man who surfed every day. He always gave Rob advice and invited him to surf.

Stu had lived and surfed in Australia as a young man and had many, many tales. He told Rob once that he met Madonna in Tynemouth Plaza and that he had managed Nigel Veitch. He told Gabe that he once cast a fishing line from the Pacific Coast Highway in his car to the sea at Cardiff by the Sea and caught a Marlin. Surfer's tales are the best. Dave Ekers once told Rob that he was chased in the sea by a sea snake in Papua New Guinea. Its head coming after him out of the water like Nessie.

Stu was a man to be admired, he surfed every day and still went on surf trips to California, Morocco and Portugal. Rob once watched him one fall try to paddle out in huge double overhead surf at Longsands. He never gave up and persevered despite the size and dangers and sheer exhilerance.

The surfers were an eclectic bunch. They were doctors,such as James a great longboarder, solicitors like Julian, teachers like Irish Simon, and everything in between. Their fashion was nothing like the Quicksilver and Vans wearing Cornish. Rob still based his hair and fashion on Jonny Marr and Bernard Sumner. Mat was uber cool and wore the latest threads well. He was from Chesterfield originally but live in Bedlington. He was a great surfer and a nice guy. Eight stones wet through. He was known as Marpet because he was so hairy [half man/half carpet , Marpet]. He used to be an A and R man for a record company but he was now in the rag trade. Mat had broken his neck at Blyth Beach in small surf but had recovered fully after a year. Gabe had done the same with his leg at Blyth.

Most of the Geordie surfers were into dance music and Titch was an accomplished DJ. The annual surf ball at the Park Hotel was all dance music. There were exceptions such as Jed who played drums for Sunset Sons and Owain who managed Sam Fender and Ben Howard.

Longsand's Beach was the epi-centre of the scene and Tynemouth Surf Co, which was owned by Hurricane was the focus as well as the waves. Hurricane was a lovely guy and an excellent surfer. He always spoke in the sea and gave non- judgemental advice. He gave Nu a hoody and t shirt as a gift when he was born. He was a graceful long boarder and a fearless short boarder. He caught anything and made surfing look easy. His Dad was one of the original Tynemouth surfers.

Chad and Nathan opened a cool Surf Shop called Rubber Soul and for a while even Rob was in negotiations with his friend, Glenn at Surfed out Surf Shop in Braunton to open a store.

The surfers mostly drank in the Turk's Head pub in Tynemouth until the Barca Art Bar opened. Mary's pictures of surf hung on the walls and Sandy worked behind the bar.

Rob had been on surf trips to the South of France with Ade and he went every year with his own family and once went to Spain driving in his 1966 VW Campervan. Rob loved the pine forests of Les Landes and the Longboard beach breaks in Biarritz in front of the Casino and the Basque's Beach. Mimizan was his families place, a trendy town centre, child friendly and a beautiful beach. It worked at low tide as did most of the Landes [and Cornish beaches] but could be rippy and fickle.

Other than France and Devon, Rob's first proper surf trip with other surfers was to Morocco. The crew was assembled; Mike the Mod, Fritz, and Gaz. The flight to Agadir took off from Liverpool airport, the boards were loaded onto the aircraft and the madness ensued. Fritz and Rob opened their litre of Vodka and drank the whole lot by ordering Tomato Juices and Coke.

They landed at Agadir Airport collected their boards and headed out through customs. They were approached by a scruffy Moroccan guy in a make shift suit. Rob had agreed to rent a car from him, but the guy wanted to do business in the dark car park. Not exactly Europcar. There sat this little white, Dacia basic saloon car. No deposit left and no driving license seen and the lads were off into the dark and fragrant Moroccan night. They drove through the darkness occasionally driving through a shanty town that was full of noise and animals with bare light bulbs. They hit the coast, turning right at a castle and headed into the desert wilderness until they reached Taghazout, a very small white housed town that Jimmy Hendrix once lived in.
They found there surf hostel at Hash Point, called Surf Berbere. The smell of faeces hit them the moment that they got out of the car. They made their way through the darkness, down the ancient passage to the rocky point. There stood a thick Moorish Moroccan studded wooden door. Rob half expected Saladin to appear. The white building was ancient and about 4 stories high. The door creaked open and a dreadlocked blonde Australian girl welcomed the lads in.

Fritz, Rob and the Mod were in a four bedroomed dorm with a random Scottish girl and Gaz was two storied up in a dorm with 16 other randomers on bunks. Gaz called it the Black Hole of Calcutta. It was too late for food at the hostel so the lads headed into town. Drinking was illegal so there were no bars. The town main street was empty. They found a place with a light on and four chairs were supplied. The only food they offered was Tagine. Four bowls arrived with Arabic style domes on top, some flat bread and a Harissa hot dip. Four Cokes arrived and the lads got stuck in. The mystery meat and bones in the watery stew was medieval.

Back at the hostel they went up to the beautiful tiled roof terrace that was lit by Moroccan lanterns. The bay was in darkness but the terrace was quite lively with other people from the hostel. The lads sat amongst the scattered cushions and were offered beers and a draw on the tack from the hookah pipe. There was a blonde South African guy with a god's body who worked for the hostel. He gave the lads tips on where to surf and said that he'd get them a couple of slabs of Flag Lager Beer. The conversation flowed with some Irish surfers and Gaz and Fritz told them the story of the Dolphin toucher of Amble.

The next morning after a huge communal breakfast of bread, eggs, fresh conserves and fruit the lads loaded up the Dacia and headed off to the break known as Crocs. They parked up at the beach on a slight cliff top. They unloaded their boards and a guy appeared upon a camel and lurked about.

As Rob fitted the fin to his Bear Longboard the guy in a Moroccan Jalaba with the camel wriggled Rob's board to check the tightness of his fin, like he was an expert. Fritz still drowsy from the night before slipped on the cliff top roof and nearly fell. He cut his foot badly in the process and a big flap of skin was hanging down. He shrugged it off and went to surf. These Peterlee boys are made out of strong stuff.

The four of them paddled out into the warm October water and after chest deep they noticed lots of little fish around them feeding up[on brown string stuff all floating on the surface as they paddled through it. It was human faeces! However, the surf was 2-3 foot and clean and they had a great day surfing this easy beach break. They got out and returned to the Demon Dacia.

As they were getting changed a hawker appeared shouting his wares as 'climate change, cacahuets'. Rob said 'I'll have a bag of those Climate changes please'. The Hawker passed over a plastic bag with crabby looking Clementine's in. He then went over and started stroking Gaz's bald head and started calling him 'Nice Head'. From this moment onwards Gaz became known as Nice Heed. The lads did buy a huge lump of resin off him and it was not the sort that you use to manufacture or repair surfboards.

That night the lads were zobbed out watching *Let the Right One in* on the communal television after eating another Tagine cooked this time at the hostel. No mystery meat. Gaz spent his second night in the room of death. Fritz put the Scottish woman's pants on the Mod's head as she was not in.

The next day the lads headed up the coast to Tamri out in the wilds. It was a huge expanse of land with a beach break. The lads pulled into the free rough land car park and Moroccan youths approached and asked for money and the guys gave them the small amount to look after the car and they disappeared.

They were getting changed behind their towels and Rob decided for a laugh that he's put on his fluorescent green mankini. He had told no one. Rob appeared from behind the car with the garment barely covering his pale body. Moroccan youths arrived from everywhere, out of bushes, sand dunes. They must have been watching like foxes.
They were shouting at Rob 'you offend us', and were pulling at his mankind. Rob was laughing and saying 'Get ya eyes off'. This made matters worse. Eventually after more money the situation calmed and Rob put his shorty wetsuit on.

The surf was hard trying to get through the white-water and the lads decided to go north and then go back in, so they wore their wetsuits in the car. They needed petrol so went in Tami town about a mile away. It was one main street with sheep's heads hanging up on stalls at the side of the road, stray dogs and a market. Rob pulled into the petrol station and the lads got out of the car. He went to the petrol pump and it had a chain around it. A guy appeared and had a vegetable oil bottle full of yellow liquid out and poured it with a funnel into the tank. Rob went to pay and realised that he's left his wallet in the car. The car had locked and Rob could see the keys on the driver's seat. So now there were 4 Geordie idiots in the middle of a North African town in wetsuits at mid day locked out of a car. A crowd started to gather and stand around them. All over a sudden a man appeared from nowhere and with one turn of a key that he had in his hand opened the car door. He didn't even stop so that the lads could thank him.

It was time for tagine on so the lads stopped at the edge of town got changed. The entered the last café and ordered 'quatrc tagine et cola'. They were approached by a western looking Moroccan in a leather jacket with a gold necklace. He warned them not to eat there and then shouted abuse in Arabic at the owner. The boys stayed and enjoyed another mystery meat, bone tagine.

Rob returned to Morocco a few years later for Mat's Birthday. This was totally different type of trip. There were eight of them and they were all far better surfers than Rob. Boaby P had rented a huge house in the middle of Tamracht, a village in the South of Morocco about 5 miles from Taghzout. It was a gorgeous huge multi story old building with Moroccan tiles and furniture inside. They had to drive through a maze of dirt streets lined with terraced houses to get to it and the local kids threw stones at their 2 cars.

Every day was up at 5.30 am, Bananas for breakfast load the car and arrive in Tamri, as it was the only place working for a dawn surf. Lunch of omelette or Tagine then another surf. By the end of the trip Rob's snoring had reduced Titch's nerves to shreds, he couldn't take anymore. Beefy and Moony weren't bothered.

Hurricane was staying with his girlfriend in a villa just outside Taghazout and the crew went to visit him. They all surfed Killers except for Rob who surfed Mysteries as it was smaller. Anchors was working but it was quick and like a gladiatorial contest watched by a baying crowd.

The last day was spent surfing a secret point break called Scabby Dogs. Boaby P caught an awesome long right. Titch and Jimmy managed to get sea urchin spines through their wetsuits and into their thighs.

Only one accident this visit. Rob drove to Taghazout to buy some resin. He ended up in an unknown guy's room where there was a wife and child. There were no seats just cushions and throws. The cooker was a large Bluet camping stove. Rob bought the gear and left. For some odd reason he drove on the left on the way back and managed to avoid a huge head on crash, just smashing the wing mirror. The lads went on further big Boaby P trips like a two week boat trip around the Maldives but Rob was not allowed to go on account of the snore factor. However, Rob's next big trip was to Portugal. Different crew again; Rob, Mike the Mod, Seamus and Big Al.

The trip started as usual in the airport bar in Newcastle and the flight was lubricated by Stella. Rob's skin was still green from the Halloween party that he had been to the night before. The crew landed in Faro and after clearing customs there was a stand advertising a golf course and free Super Bok Beer. The lads stood there for a further 90 minutes drinking free ale. They got to the Surf Algarve hostel and dumped their stuff and out again.

The first bar was an Irish bar owned by a guy called Derek. Something then happened that Rob doubted ever happened. When he was working in Ashington Rob had to give evidence about a dodgy teacher called Roger. The lads were standing at the bar and Roger walked in. Rob had to make a quick exit.

The lads discovered The Tavern, The Three Monkey's Bar and the Red Eye Bar. In the morning they were hanging. They surfed Porto de Mos, it was 3 foot and high tide. They went to paddle out and immediately a wave like a claw grabbed Mike and threw him back onto the beach like a ship wrecked victim. Rob caught a great right on his Surf Tech Board that he'd recently bought from Mick the Sparky in Tynemouth. A fast hollow long ride that made Rob's heart race. Rob paddled back out to the outside and spewed into the sea, carrots and lumps all around him. A Portuguese middle aged surfer looked over in disgust. Rob paddled in and fell asleep on the beach in his wetsuit like a seal.

Over the next few days the lads discovered the West Coast breaks and one day they had a great day surfing Cordoama. They were buzzing afterwards after a 5 foot and clean session. They drove back to Lagos and had a few well-earned Crystal Beers at a Euro each as an après surf. They were elated and the atmosphere and camaraderie was overwhelming. It was going to be a good night.

The night began well, on the vinho tinto and a piri piri chicken meal in the harbour side. The lads then hit the Shaka Bar. They were putting requests on for *Gay Bar* by Electric Six and dancing around especially Seamus who did the Irish Jig up and down the bar to the Irish Rover. The lads were steaming drunk. Big Al was approached by a dirty fingered Portuguese man asking if the wanted any Charlie? The lads chipped in and bought a big bag. Al went to the toilets first for a toot and he said it was rubbish, next Rob and he passed the bag to Mike.

Mike returned from the toilets and carried on dancing. Rob said to Mike 'Where's the gear?'

Mike said 'What gear?' He had eaten the lot including the bag!

An Irish girl who was in her early twenties approached Rob and told him that he was gorgeous. Rob just showed her his wedding ring. He wouldn't have done that before Almond Eyes.

The next day there was a huge black cloud hanging over the lads in the hostel. Apparently, they had got back late and taken their clothes off and played *Gay Bar* full blast and danced around the dorms, scaring the Russian guests. Rob had also gone upstairs to the communal fridge and eaten all of the German Vegan girl's prepared lunch for her surf trip the next day.

A sullen drive along the south coast to Tonal and the waves were overhead and breaking on the shore. Rob did not go in but the rest did. Seamus who had been surfing really well caught an overhead wave and came down the face and over the lip. Rob lay on the beach puking.

Rob went on a surf trip to South Wales with Boaby P, Mike the Mod and Nice Heed. Rob booked an army bell tent on a farm. It was blooming freezing in March and there was snow on the ground. Mike tried to make coffee in the morning and lit the gas cooker upsides down and nearly blew them all up. Rob had a cocked breakfast with cockles and spewed it up. On the way back on the M5 an articulated lorry came off the overhead bridge and onto the carriageway and could have killed them all! Nice Head gave the driver medical attention.

Chapter 12

Change, change. Rob at the age of 48 began playing First Team Rugby for Winlaton Vulcans RFC. They were like Anstey, not just because they wore all black, but because they were proper working class blokes, who played hard, very hard and drank hard. Rob loved playing for them and ending his career with them. He even got the chance to play against his old club Rockcliff and play well and beat them

Rob started a new job in a lovely school in Gateshead. He thought that he would finish his career at the school. Lovely staff, lovely kids and his rugby team did very well .They got to the school's North championships and always thrashed the Emmanuel Foundation. There were some flaws with the school. It had merged with another school and some of the parents were disgruntled and moved their kids to a nearby Catholic School thus slicing off the top end students.

The other flaw was the finances. The school was heavily in debt and financially it couldn't even afford books and pens. It made about 30 staff redundant per year over 3 years and Rob thought that after 3 good years he'd better look for something else or be on the redundancy list, even though he's just been promoted to Assistant head of Faculty.

There had been a strange move in pedagogical thinking over the past 5 years, everyone was Kagen Krazy, which was a style of teaching and learning that involved playing games and had snazzy titles like think, pair share. Give one, get one. The first time Rob came across this was in Ashington where a new careerist wonder suited boy used all the jargon. He's probably a head teacher now.

The problem with Kagen was that nothing was in the kid's books. Just as each period looks to another for a complete opposite change. The thing that followed Kagen was progress over time in books and textbook and worksheet work. Didactic teaching, Knowledge organisers and facts.

I suppose it was at this point Rob saw the madness in it all and was jaded by it a little. But he got a new job as head of department in darkest Sunderland. The day after he had got the job he went for a beer in the Left Luggage Lounge in Monkseaton and a mate of Mike the Mods said' No matter what you do, divvunt gan there, the head's crazy'.

Rob started his new job, regardless. Over the previous 10 years the school had increased its GCSE results under a new head teacher. Who was ruthless and driven by what she saw as doing the best for the students, but she'd somehow lost context. This was largely done by playing around with courses that were easier or modular like the igces which they did in every subject and it was intended for students who had English as a second language. Of course, when the government stopped this course the results dipped and the Senior Leadership Team were so inflated by their own egos they could not figure out why and began the old blame game to the teachers. Rob knew his job was a difficult one because the previous golden boy careerist suited head of department had left with good results through the igcse but left knowing that they would drop dramatically for the next incumbent.

To make matters worse he had taught the students the wrong specification for over a year along with the other Historian, the over dramatic and teary, Breakdown Annie. Rob observed before making any changes but everything was a mess. Annie fancied herself as Head of Department and had tampered and adjusted the schemes of work. It was a mess. Sunderland Football Club came in every lunchtime and just let the kids run wild on the all-weather pitch with no structure, kicking balls everywhere. The staff were mostly Teach First students because that way the school could get cheap labour. This is all too often the case.

The school had an odd student voice that involved them voting for teacher of the month. Bizarrely. Rob won it every month so the Senior Leadership took Rob's name off the list. The school made every teacher train for Team Teach and there was lots of restraining students. Nearly as much as in the Pupil Referral Unit. Students who kicked off were often locked out into the yard. It was an odd place the staff were petrified of the head who often made off the cuff job threats to the staff. The staff all called her behind her back.

There was a bullish assistant head called Belinda from some Southern hemisphere Country, who crawled around the head but spoke ill of her behind her back. If she could do that to her, she will do that to anyone, it's her management style... When Breakdown Annie went on the sick with stress, claiming she had no support for Rob she began to gather evidence about Rob. They got an adviser in from Durham who looked like Grotbags from the Pink Windmill and she even wore odd socks. Rob could not take her serious and laughed at he comments, which angered her even more. She was all for chalk and talk, facts and knowledge regurgitation. She was not an academic.

Rob had had enough. Twenty Five years and out. He could not bear to put his young family under any more strain. He was drinking more and making himself ill. He was too long in the tooth to play games with backstabbing Annie who only cared about herself or careerists, so he just resigned. It's funny that often the people who have the least to offer always have the best opinion of themselves.

What's the point if, the school holidays are just spent worrying, if your line manager is a liar, if your department do anything to get your job, if there's no trust, if you think that the ethos is immoral?

Maybe he had always been a rubbish teacher anyways. He was once told that he'd become an ass when he became a teacher. He got himself a job as an accountant on half the salary.

He felt like a failure but Almond Eyes praised him and he could sleep at night and care for his kids.

Printed in Poland
by Amazon Fulfillment
Poland Sp. z o.o., Wrocław